Katie's New Shoes

by Fran Manushkin

illustrated by Tammie Lyon

PICTURE WINDOW BOOKS
a capstone imprint

Katie Woo is published by Picture Window Books,
1710 Roe Crest Drive
North Mankato, Minnesota 56003
www.capstonepub.com

Text © 2012 Fran Manushkin
Illustrations © 2012 Picture Window Books

Library of Congress Cataloging-in-Publication Data
Manushkin, Fran.
 Katie's new shoes / by Fran Manushkin; illustrated by Tammie Lyon.
    p. cm. — (Katie Woo)
 Summary: When Katie outgrows her shoes, she and her friends JoJo and Pedro go to the shoe store with their mothers.
 ISBN 978-1-4048-6519-8 (library binding)
 ISBN 978-1-4048-6855-7 (pbk.)
 [1. Shoes—Fiction. 2. Shopping—Fiction. 3. Chinese Americans—Fiction.] I. Lyon, Tammie, ill. II. Title.
 PZ7.M3195Kcn 2011
 [E]—dc22   2011005489

Art Director: Kay Fraser
Graphic Designer: Emily Harris

Printed in the United States of America in Stevens Point, Wisconsin.
112011
006455R

Table of Contents

Chapter 1

Ouch!

"Something is wrong with
my toes," said Katie Woo.
"They hurt when I walk or
run. They hurt when I wiggle
them, too. I think I have the
ouches!"

"Your toes are fine," said Katie's mom. "Your shoes are the problem. You are growing so fast, they don't fit you anymore."

"Uh-oh," Katie groaned. "I'd better slow down! If I keep growing fast, my feet will be as big as a horse's or an elephant's! "

"No way," said Katie's

dad. "I promise you will

always have human feet."

"Good!" said Katie. "I like

being human."

Katie told Pedro and JoJo

about her big toes.

"My toes are so big, they

poked a hole in my shoes,"

bragged Pedro.

"My shoes are

falling apart, too,"

said JoJo.

Chapter 2

Shoe Shopping

Kalie, Pedro, and JoJo
went to Super Shoes with
their moms. The store was
huge!

It had sneakers and boots and party shoes. It had shoes with sparkles and shoes with wheels.

It had boxes of shoes all the way to the ceiling!

"I want speedy shoes,"
said Pedro. "Shoes for
running fast!"

"I want bouncy shoes,"
said JoJo. "Shoes for jumping
high!"

Katie said, "I want shoes
with pizzazz!"

"What's pizzazz?" asked
JoJo.

"It means they look great!"
said Katie.

"We want different

things," said JoJo. "I'm

sure we won't like the same

shoes."

Katie tried on shoes with
buckles and bows and straps
and zippers. Soon the boxes
were piled high.

"None of these has
pizzazz," said Katie, sighing.

"I wish I were a cat," said
Katie. "Cats have their own
furry shoes."

"But cats have to eat
mice," said Katie's mom.

"Yuck!" Katie moaned.
"Never mind!"

A little girl near Katie was
crying.

"She doesn't like trying on
shoes," said her mom.

"Shoes can be fun!" Katie
told the little girl. But the girl
kept crying.

"Look!" Katie said to the girl.

She put baby shoes on her hands and made them dance and talk like puppets.

The little girl giggled and
let her mom try on some
shoes.

"Thank you!" said the
mom as Katie danced away.

Chapter 3

The Perfect Shoes

"Will I ever find the

perfect shoes?" Katie sighed.

"Yes," said her mom. "Just

like Cinderella!"

Katie tried on her sixteenth pair of shoes. "Hey," she said, smiling. "These are IT!"

"Do they have pizzazz?" asked Katie's mom.

"Tons of it!" said Katie. "And my toes are happy!"

Katie danced over to JoJo,

saying, "Look! I found the

perfect shoes."

"Surprise!" JoJo said. "We

picked the same ones."

"Wow!" Katie said. "We

both have pizzazz."

"Sure," agreed Pedro. "But

my shoes are the fastest."

"Race you home!" Katie

said. And off they went!

They passed the little girl. She was showing off her new shoes.

"Shoes are fun!" she shouted.

Katie agreed. "When my toes are happy, I'm happy."

And she kept on running!

About the Author

Fran Manushkin is the author of many
popular picture books, including *How Mama
Brought the Spring: Baby, Come Out!: Latkes
and Applesauce: A Hanukkah Story:* and *The
Tushy Book.* There is a real Katie Woo — she's
Fran's great-niece — but she never gets in
half the trouble of the Katie Woo in the books.
Fran writes on her beloved Mac computer in New York City,
without the help of her two naughty cats, Miss Chippie
and Goldy.

About the Illustrator

Tammie Lyon began her love for drawing
at a young age while sitting at the
kitchen table with her dad. She continued
her love of art and eventually attended
the Columbus College of Art and Design,
where she earned a bachelors degree in fine
art. After a brief career as a professional
ballet dancer, she decided to devote herself full time to
illustration. Today she lives with her husband, Lee, in Cincinnati,
Ohio. Her dogs, Gus and Dudley, keep her company as she works
in her studio.

Glossary

bragged (BRAGGD)—talked in a boastful way about how good you are at something

buckles (BUHK-uhlz)—metal fastenings on shoes

ceiling (SEE-ling)—the upper surface inside a room

Cinderella (sin-der-REL-lah)—the main character of a fairy tale in which she is helped by a fairy Godmother

human (HYOO-muhn)—a person

pizzazz (pih-ZAZ)—attractive style or flair

sneakers (SNEE-kurz)—athletic shoes with rubber soles

sparkles (SPAR-kulz)—glitter

wiggle (WIG-uhl)—to make small movements from side to side or up and down

Discussion Questions

1. Why did Katie want shoes with pizzazz? Would you like shoes with pizzazz?

2. Why was the little girl so upset? How did Katie help her?

3. Were you surprised that Katie and JoJo picked out the same shoes? Why or why not?

Writing Prompts

1. Make a list of five words that describe your favorite pair of shoes.

2. Pedro wanted shoes to run in, and JoJo wanted shoes to jump in. What do you like to do in your shoes? Write a paragraph about it.

3. What if you didn't have any shoes? Write a story about a shoeless adventure. Describe how your feet feel. Do you like it? Does it hurt?

Reuse Your Shoes!

When you outgrow or wear out your shoes, you don't have to throw them out. If they are still in good condition, give them to a thrift store. (Maybe someone else can use them.) But if they are pretty worn, this project will give your shoes new life.

Pretty Planters

What you need:

• a pair of old shoes

• a drill with small drill bit

• potting soil

• flower seeds or a small plant

What you do:

1. Ask a grown-up to drill several small holes in the bottoms of the shoes. These holes will let water drain out to help keep your plants healthy.

2. Fill the toe of the shoe with potting soil. Pack it in firmly. If you are using seeds, move on to step three. If you are using a plant, skip to step four.

3. Fill the rest of the shoe with potting soil. Plant your seeds according to the directions on the package. Follow the directions for how to care for the seeds, and soon you will have a shoe full of flowers!

4. Place some soil in the heel of the shoe, leaving room for your plant. Carefully, place the plant in, adding more soil around it to secure it in place. Water it thoroughly.

Water your planters every day, and enjoy the pretty flowers. This makes a very nice gift for your mom or grandma, too!

THE FUN DOESN'T STOP HERE!

Discover more at www.capstonekids.com

- ♥ Videos & Contests
- ❀ Games & Puzzles
- ♥ Friends & Favorites
- ❀ Authors & Illustrators

Find cool websites and more books like this one at www.facthound.com. Just type in the Book ID: **9781404865198** and you're ready to go!